DC COMICS™

TALES OF THE
BATCAVE

THE CLOWN PRINCE
OF CARDS

by
MICHAEL DAHL

illustrated by
LUCIANO VECCHIO

Batman created by
BOB KANE WITH BILL FINGER

STONE ARCH BOOKS
a capstone imprint

Published by Stone Arch Books in 2016
A Capstone Imprint
1710 Roe Crest Drive
North Mankato, Minnesota 56003
www.mycapstone.com

STAR36188

Library of Congress Cataloging-in-Publication Data is available on the Library of
Congress website.

ISBN: 978-1-4965-4013-3 (library binding)
ISBN: 978-1-4965-4017-1 (paperback)
ISBN: 978-1-4965-4021-8 (eBook PDF)

Summary: When high-stakes hijinks grip Gotham City, Batman and Robin jump into
action. They soon learn the Joker is pulling off high-rise heists with the help of a giant
flying playing card. Can the Dynamic Duo take down the Clown Prince of Crime with
the ace up their sleeves? Or will the Joker's wild ride lift the super-villain to new
criminal heights?

Editor: Christopher Harbo
Designer: Bob Lentz
Production Specialist: Kathy McColley

Printed and bound in the USA.
009625F16

TABLE OF CONTENTS

This is the BATCAVE.

GIANT
JOKER
PLAYING
CARD

It is the secret headquarters of Batman and his crime-fighting partner, Robin.

Hundreds of trophies, awards, and souvenirs fill the Batcave's hidden rooms. Each one tells a story of danger, villainy, and victory.

This is the tale of a giant Joker playing card! And why this trophy now stands in the Batcave . . .

CHAPTER 1

THE KING'S TREASURE

Two dark figures stand atop Gotham City's tallest skyscraper.

They swoop through the darkness on long ropes, and swing through a tall open window.

"Batman! Robin!" shouts a man, as they drop inside a fancy hotel room.

"Evening, Commissioner Gordon," says Batman. "Any clues to the missing treasure?"

"Not yet," Gordon says. "But thanks for sending Ace to help us out."

A large dog sniffs the rugs and furniture. It is Ace, the Bat-Hound. He is working undercover without his mask and cape.

"How could a thief steal the national treasure of Prankistan from this penthouse?" says Gordon.

"And from the tallest building in the city!"
says the Boy Wonder. "It's a puzzle."

"Did you post guards in the elevators?"
Batman asks.

"Yes," says Gordon. "I even put security on the roof. No one has been seen up there except you tonight."

"This looks like an impossible crime!" Robin says, punching his glove.

CHAPTER 2

THE RULER'S EXIT

Another man bursts into the room. He wears a gold suit and a turban covered in jewels.

"Dynamic Duo!" he cries. "You are finding the treasure, no?"

"Don't worry, your Highness," says Gordon. "No one can hide from Batman and Robin."

"You must help me," begs the King of Prankistan. "The royal cobra has been in my family for years."

"A snake is the national treasure?" whispers Robin to Batman.

"The emperor cobra of Prankistan is the rarest snake in the world," Batman whispers back.

The Bat-Hound barks from another room.

The crime fighters and Commissioner Gordon quickly follow the dog's signal.

"What did you find, Ace?" says Robin.

The Bat-Hound has his paws on an open windowsill.

"The thief must have left by this window," says Batman.

"But how?" says Gordon. "We're on the top floor!"

YAAAAAAAAA!

A scream comes from the King of Prankistan in the other room.

Robin and Ace race back.

They find an empty room. A jeweled turban lies on the floor.

"The King has vanished!" cries the Boy Wonder.

Ace sniffs at the turban. Batman rushes to the open window and peers into the darkness.

Suddenly, a loud alarm blares from several blocks away.

"Another robbery!" cries Batman.

CHAPTER 3

THE QUEEN'S CROWN

The Batmobile roars through the city streets tracking the wail of the alarm.

The car screeches to a stop as two security guards hail the heroes.

"Look!" says one of the guards. He points toward the top of a nearby building.

19

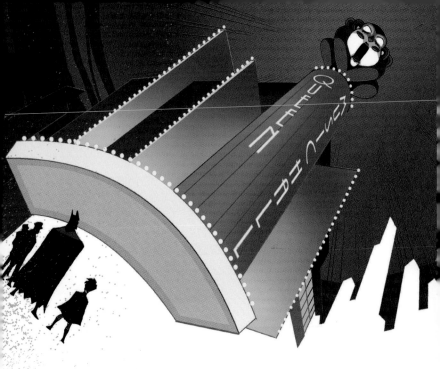

"The crown on the Queen Music Hall statue has vanished!" Robin cries.

"Another royal treasure gone!" says Batman.

"And another high-level robbery," says Robin.

"High is right," says one of the guards. "That sign is one hundred feet above the ground."

"Is there a way up?" asks Batman.

"Only a metal spiral staircase," answers the guard. "And I was guarding the locked gate in front of it."

Suddenly, Ace the Bat-Hound begins to growl.

"Listen," says a guard. "Do you hear that humming sound?"

A sudden shadow passes swiftly above their heads.

A moment later another alarm shrieks several blocks away.

"I sense a crime wave in the air," says Batman.

The Dynamic Duo and Ace rush back to
the Batmobile.

The vehicle roars to life and rockets toward
the new alarm.

CHAPTER 4

THE JOKER'S WILD

"There it is, Batman!" cries Robin, pointing. "By the Regal department store's tenth floor!"

A flickering shape hovers high in the air near a broken window.

"Don't tell me that's a flying carpet!" says Robin.

"And it's next to the jewelry showroom!"
says Batman.

A figure steps out of the broken window and
onto the floating rectangle.

The shape glides down toward the Batmobile.

A weird laugh echoes through the night.

HAHAHAHAHA!

"The Joker!" shouts Robin.

"People have been calling me a card for years!" he shrieks. "So I finally went and made one of my own!"

The Joker stands on a giant playing card. A Joker!

"I've become quite the flying ace," he laughs.

The villain swoops toward the Dynamic Duo.
Batman and Robin leap out of the way.

Ace jumps out of the Batmobile and dashes
down an alley.

"I'm good at *attracting* attention," chuckles the Joker, rising above the heroes again. "But I hope I don't *repulse* you."

"Attract. Repulse," says the Dark Knight. "The Joker's flying card must be powered by an electromagnet."

"Its humming engine pushes and pulls him between any buildings built with metal," adds the Boy Wonder.

Batman and Robin pull Batarangs from their belts. They aim for the Clown Prince of Crime.

"Careful, Dynamic Duo!" warns the villain. "If you pull me down, you'll break my crown!"

The Joker flies low. The heroes glimpse a figure in a gold suit lying next to the villain.

"The King of Prankistan!" shouts Robin.

"Stand down, Robin," orders Batman.
"We can't put the king's life in danger."

CHAPTER 5

THE UPPER HAND

The Joker stands high above Batman and Robin. His flying card hovers near the Regal building.

"Holding the king gives me the upper hand!" crows the criminal.

HAHAHAHAHAHAHA!

"Now I'm off to my next —"

A shadow appears at one of the building's windows. It growls and leaps at the Joker.

The villain is carried over the edge of his card and onto a nearby fire escape.

"It's Ace!" says Robin. "Good boy!"

With the Joker caught by Ace, the card floats harmlessly to the ground.

"The king is safe," says Batman with a smile. "Thanks to Ace, we'll recover the missing crown and the royal cobra."

"That crooked clown," says Robin. "He should have known an Ace always beats a Joker!"

35

"Batman, can we keep the Joker's flying card in the Batcave?"

"As a reminder of how we dealt with that villain?"

"Yeah, it would be a shame to discard it."

"Suits me, Boy Wonder. How about you, Ace?"

"Woof! Woof!"

GLOSSARY

attract (uh-TRAKT)—to pull something toward something else

card (KARD)—a clownishly amusing person; also a stiff, rectangular piece of paper used in games

commissioner (kuh-MI-shuh-nuhr)—a person who is in charge of a government department

electromagnet (i-lek-troh-MAG-nuht)—a temporary magnet created by an electric current

emperor (EM-puhr-uhr)—the leader of a country or group of countries

hover (HUHV-ur)—to remain in one place in the air

penthouse (PENT-houss)—an apartment located on the top floor of a tall building

repulse (ri-PUHLSS)—to drive or force back

security (si-KYOOR-i-tee)—guards who watch over or protect something

turban (TUR-buhn)—a head covering made by winding a long scarf around the head or around a cap

Discuss

1. Robin says the Joker's flying card uses magnetic power to push and pull him through the air. Do you know what he means?

2. The Joker likes to follow a theme when he commits his crimes. Based on the names of what he stole and where he went, can you figure out his theme this time?

3. The Dynamic Duo and Ace work together as a team. Do you think Batman and Robin could have captured the Joker without Ace's help?

Write

1. The Joker uses his new invention, the flying card, to move around Gotham City. What would you do with a flying device like that? Write a paragraph about it.

2. The King of Prankistan's royal pet is a cobra. If you could have an unusual pet, what would you choose? Describe it and write how you would take care of it.

3. The heroes in this story are sometimes called by other names: the Dynamic Duo, the Dark Knight, and the Boy Wonder. If you were a super hero, what would your powers be? And what nicknames would you have?

Author

Michael Dahl is the prolific author of the best-selling *Goodnight Baseball* picture book and more than 200 other books for children and young adults. He has won the AEP Distinguished Achievement Award three times for his nonfiction, a Teachers' Choice Award from *Learning* magazine, and a Seal of Excellence from the Creative Child Awards. He is also the author of the Hocus Pocus Hotel mystery series and the Dragonblood books. Dahl currently lives in Minneapolis, Minnesota.

Illustrator

Luciano Vecchio was born in 1982 and is based in Buenos Aires, Argentina. Freelance artist for many projects at Marvel and DC Comics, his work has been seen in print and online around the world. He has illustrated many DC Super Heroes books for Capstone, and some of his recent comic work includes *Beware the Batman*, *Green Lantern: The Animated Series*, *Young Justice*, *Ultimate Spider-Man*, and his creator owned web-comic, *Sereno*.